THIS BOOK BELONGS TO...

BOUBLES GRAND HOTEL

# Mr Badger

## and the

# Difficult Duchess

Leigh HOBBS

**ALLEN&UNWIN**

*For Andrea Reece*

First published in 2011
Copyright © Leigh Hobbs 2011

Allen & Unwin
83 Alexander Street
Crows Nest NSW 2065 Australia
Phone: (61 2) 8425 0100
Fax: (61 2) 9906 2218
Email: info@allenandunwin.com
Web: www.allenandunwin.com

Cataloguing-in-Publication entry is available from
the National Library of Australia
www.trove.nla.gov.au

ISBN 978 1 74237 419 2

Cover and text design by Sandra Nobes
Set in 15 pt Cochin by Sandra Nobes
Author photograph by Peter Gray
Printed in August 2012 by the SOS Print + Media Group (Aust) Pty Ltd
at 65 Burrows Road Alexandria NSW 2015

*The author wishes to acknowledge the invaluable assistance of the Badger gang,
Erica Wagner, Sandra Nobes and Elise Jones.*

3 5 7 9 10 8 6 4 2

# Contents

# CHAPTER 1

# Special Guests

Mr Badger had excellent manners plus a great deal of patience. But you probably knew that already.

This is why he didn't *just* manage special events at the Boubles Grand Hotel (pronounced *Boublay*). Mr Badger was also the Manager of Special Guests – and sometimes *very* special guests.

Special guests weren't treated all that differently to anyone else. It was just that film stars and princesses, kings, queens and famous orchestra conductors often caused a fuss because people wanted to stare at them and point. Or ask them for their autographs while they ate their dinner in the Boubles Grand Hotel Dining Room, or enjoyed afternoon tea in the lounge.

And one must say that special guests *were* often quite demanding when it came to their rooms and meals, just for a start. Celebrities are used to being the centre of attention, so naturally when they stayed at the Boubles Grand Hotel they expected a lot of looking after.

Some *extremely* important people wore disguises in the dining room. Others preferred to keep out of reach

*Some guests went to a lot of trouble so as not to be recognised.*

and stay in their rooms, away from their fans and the staring public. They were the ones who didn't like being looked at.

Mr Badger knew this from experience. After all, you couldn't possibly have people interrupting a king or queen to ask for their autograph while they were eating breakfast. Or, worse still, pestering them to pose for a photograph while they were holding a piece of toast or eating cornflakes.

## CHAPTER 2

# Mr Badger's Diary

Each guest at the Boubles Grand
Hotel was important, and every
one of them was treated with the
utmost courtesy by the staff.

Still, Miss Pims, Mr Badger's
helpful assistant, always left a note in
Mr Badger's diary if someone special –
say a duke, or a famous actor, or the
latest celebrity – had reserved a suite
at the Boubles Grand Hotel.

5

On this particular day, Mr Badger arrived for work in the early hours as he always did and opened his diary to study the coming day's events.

Every day there were all manner of things for Mr Badger to do and check and order and look at. And every one of them was carefully noted in his diary by Miss Pims.

*Every morning Mr Badger checked his diary.*

For instance, today the diary said:
*1. Order flowers for the Philatelic Society Annual Dinner to be held tonight in the Grand Ballroom.* (Sir Cecil and Lady Celia were the patrons of the stamp-collectors' society. This was the members' chance to meet and swap stamps.)

7

2. *Clean the chandelier and polish the floors in the Grand Ballroom.*

3. *Wipe Algernon's case.* (As usual, Algernon the ape's case was covered in small marks from the many little hands and noses that pressed against the glass each day. Children adored Algernon.)

Of course, Mr Badger didn't *personally* lower the chandelier and dust the crystal and climb up a ladder to replace the light bulbs, or polish the floors and collect and wash the dishes from the dining room after morning and afternoon tea every day.

Oh no, no, no. There were trained staff who did all of that.

However, Mr Badger *did* give the orders and do the supervising. Every task had to be completed to a very high standard – the Boubles Grand Hotel standard – and it was most important that everything be done without any fuss. Sir Cecil and Lady Celia Smothers-Carruthers, the owners of the Boubles Grand Hotel, insisted on it.

*Sir Cecil and Lady Celia Smothers-Carruthers.*

'Keep up the good work,' Sir Cecil would say whenever he passed Mr Badger in the corridor.

Anyway, according to Mr Badger's diary, there were no celebrities booked into the Boubles Grand Hotel today. Not even a princess for afternoon tea.

Miss Pims arrived at work to find Mr Badger leaning back in his chair.

'Good morning, Mr Badger!' she said cheerfully.

'And good morning to you, too,' replied Mr Badger. 'I've checked your diary entries and there seems to be nothing out of the ordinary. I'm looking forward to concentrating on tonight's special event. It promises to be quite an occasion.'

# CHAPTER 3

# An Unexpected Guest

A telephone call soon after informed Mr Badger that a special guest had arrived after all.

'Mr Badger, sir,' said a trembling voice. 'It's Robert in reception. We have a guest, the Duchess de la Dodo, and she insists on taking the Royal Suite.'

'I don't recall seeing a *duchess* in my diary,' said Mr Badger, looking at Miss Pims, who in turn peered at the open page with 'today' at the top.

'According to this there is definitely no duchess due today,' said Miss Pims, nodding her head and raising her eyebrows.

Now, the Royal Suite was always kept ready in case a foreign monarch came to stay while on an official visit to London.

Occasionally, too, if local royalty dropped in for a late-night supper, Mr Badger would make arrangements for them to stay overnight in the Royal Suite – rather than have them go all the way back to the palace and troubling the guards with unlocking and locking innumerable gates and doors.

15

That meant, of course, that the lucky prince or princess would then be free to relax, have a bubble bath and enjoy a famous Boubles Grand Hotel hot chocolate before turning in.

Even though they were very busy, and her grace didn't have a reservation, Mr Badger and Miss Pims went downstairs straight away to personally welcome the Duchess de la Dodo. But neither of them was prepared for what was awaiting them at the reception desk.

It was a tall woman. In fact, not just a *tall* woman but an *extremely* tall woman. Her hair was piled up high on her head, which made her look even taller. She was wearing large sunglasses and looked very mysterious.

'Welcome, your grace,' said Mr Badger politely, only just managing to conceal his surprise. To see her face, Mr Badger had to bend his head right back.

The Duchess turned and with a majestic sweep of her arm snarled a haughty, 'How do you do?'

She had no luggage, just a large handbag.

'We have made the Royal Suite available for your grace,' said Mr Badger. 'If there is anything at all extra that you need during your stay, please let us know. How long shall we have the pleasure of your company?'

'Oh, a month or maybe two,' replied the voice from above.

*Rather troubling news*, thought Mr Badger, polishing his glasses.

'That will be all, my good man,' said the Duchess. Then she reached down and, with a *tap*, *tap*, *tap*, she patted Mr Badger on the head.

## CHAPTER 4

# A Guest in Distress

Mr Badger was a little concerned. 'Where will the Queen sleep if she drops in one evening and wants to stay overnight?' he said to Miss Pims on the way back to their office, his furry brow furrowing.

But for now Mr Badger put all thoughts of the Duchess aside as he started on his list of things to do. First he had to order the flowers for that evening's extra-special event.

21

Just then the telephone rang. Once again, it was Robert from reception.

'I'm terribly sorry, sir, but her grace is in trouble.'

'Oh dear, we are on our way,' said Mr Badger. 'I'm afraid our morning tasks will have to wait, Miss Pims.'

On nearing reception, Mr Badger and Miss Pims were presented with a most peculiar sight. For there in the lift on the left were a pair of legs and a body that extended up, then disappeared out of sight. Worryingly, on the other side of the lift, looking out from the top, was an upside-down head.

It was her grace, the Duchess de la
Dodo. She was stuck firmly in the lift.
    'Good heavens,' said Miss Pims,
stifling a gasp.

Others may have panicked, but not Mr Badger. Her grace, the Duchess de la Dodo, was a guest in distress, and this was a situation that demanded a cool head. Mr Badger summoned the fire brigade, who arrived minus bells and sirens. Then he instructed the Boubles Grand Hotel Orchestra to strike up some jolly music during morning tea so as to divert attention away from reception.

*'Is this the fire brigade?'*

While the other guests were happily
distracted, dancing in the dining room,
the Duchess was carefully unfolded
by the fire fighters and removed from
the lift.

Then she was carted upstairs in
a large sedan chair that Sir Cecil
had found abandoned in France and
Mr Badger kept at the ready for
emergencies.

# CHAPTER 5

## The Demanding Duchess

No sooner had her grace been safely delivered to the Royal Suite than Mr Badger, deep in discussion with the florist, was notified that there was another call from reception.

'Her grace has complained that the bed is too short,' said Robert.

Mr Badger, never one to get flustered, made his way up, up, up to the top floor and tapped on the door.

'*Entrez*,' said a frosty voice. Fortunately Mr Badger knew a little French, and so he entered the room.

The Duchess was resting, her extra-long legs hanging over and off the end of the bed.

'Well, your grace, this just won't do,' said Mr Badger with considerable aplomb.

'My thoughts exactly,' responded the long figure grumpily, as she slurped on a milkshake.

Mr Badger picked up the telephone and made a quick call.

Within minutes, a cluster of Boubles Grand Hotel handymen were at the door of the Royal Suite, carrying a bed.

Once inside – and only then with the Duchess's permission, of course – they lifted her amazingly straight legs and

*'Gently now, chaps,' said Mr Badger.*

(under Mr Badger's supervision) slid the extra bed in beneath her dainty feet.

The Duchess didn't need to lift a finger.

'Wonderful,' said Mr Badger. 'Thank you, gentlemen.'

There were no thanks from the Duchess de la Dodo, though. She was busy gulping down chocolates, having finished her milkshake.

# CHAPTER 6

## The Special Guest's Requests

With the Duchess's comfort ensured, Mr Badger returned downstairs. He needed to oversee the re-hanging of the recently cleaned Boubles Grand Hotel Ballroom chandelier and inspect the splendidly re-polished parquetry floor. It was so shiny that Miss Pims and Mr Badger could see their faces reflected in it.

Thanks to Miss Pims' planning and Mr Badger's expert organising skills, preparations for the stamp-collectors' dinner were under control and running smoothly.

Unfortunately, the atmosphere in the hotel kitchen was far from relaxed.

Those in charge of room service, and in turn the kitchen staff, were finding it difficult to keep up with a flood of requests. And every request came from the special guest in the Royal Suite.

For example, the Duchess had ordered: imported Belgian chocolate-chip ice-cream; a Scottish sponge cake, which had to be flown all the way down from Edinburgh by helicopter; and lots of lime-flavoured Latvian lemonade – all to be supplied 'on the double'.

And, everything was demanded and received without a single 'please' or 'thank you'.

Up and down, up and down stairways and into lifts staggered the Boubles Grand Hotel staff with a seemingly endless procession of sweets and treats.

The Duchess even sent a bellboy out for pizzas!

'I'll attend to it immediately, sir,' said Mr Badger to a disgruntled guest who complained that the Boubles Grand Hotel smelt like a pizza parlour.

It seemed to some that the hotel was looking after just one guest.

It wasn't only food that the Duchess de la Dodo was ordering, either. She demanded many toys and games be delivered to her room quick smart – not to mention three television sets for her suite. Apparently there were three programs on at the same time on different channels, and she didn't want to miss a thing.

'I must admit her grace *is* a rather demanding guest,' said Mr Badger to Miss Pims after supervising the installation of the third television.

'Hmm, to say the least,' came the reply.

*The Duchess was making the most of her stay at the Boubles Grand Hotel.*

38

# CHAPTER 7

## Stamps Galore

By now it was late afternoon and the Boubles Grand Hotel foyer was filling with eager stamp-collectors carrying their collections.

*Some philatelists swapped stories in the foyer.*

They were a rather shy lot, though
this had never stopped them from
having a wonderful – if quiet – time
at their annual get-together. It was a
chance to see each other's stamps and
maybe to do some serious swapping.
For many, this was the one evening
in the year when their most precious
stamps were revealed to other collectors.

Mr Badger and Miss Pims watched
as guests streamed through the foyer
into the Boubles Grand Hotel Ballroom.
Mr Badger quietly gave instructions,
greeted people, checked name cards
and places, and made sure guests were
shown to their correct tables. Most
importantly, he did his best to make
everyone feel welcome.

*Philatelists were filling the foyer.*

*Sir Cecil was always ready for a chat.*

'Good evening, Sir Cecil – and
how are we tonight, Lady Celia?'
said Mr Badger as the Smothers-
Carrutherses were escorted to their
VIP table. It was a well-kept secret,
but Sir Cecil and Lady Celia weren't
interested in stamps at all; nonetheless,
they were honoured to be patrons, and
never missed a dinner. Especially as the
Boubles Grand Hotel was like a second
home to the Philatelic Society.

44

Upstairs in the Royal Suite, the
Duchess had also been very busy. She'd
insisted on ordering every last luxury
that the hotel could offer, all the while
never once removing her dark glasses.

Meanwhile, downstairs, the kitchen
was still on red alert, as her grace hadn't
stopped eating since she'd arrived.

Now, though, with the sun going
down and the lights outside going on,
the Duchess was getting bored in her
Royal Suite.

45

There was nothing of interest on any of the televisions, so her grace made yet another call to room service.

'Send up the bellboys with my sedan chair,' she said. 'I wish to go downstairs.'

46

# CHAPTER 8

## An Unexpected Entrance

In the Boubles Grand Hotel Ballroom, a speech had been made by the President of the Philatelic Society and the stamp-collectors were enjoying their dinner, exchanging sensational stamp stories and swapping feverishly. Mr Badger had turned the air-conditioning off so as not to cause the guests discomfort, just in case the breeze ruffled the pages of their precious albums and unhinged the contents.

Suddenly, a hush fell upon the
room and all eyes turned towards an
extraordinarily tall figure with a curled
lip wearing sunglasses standing at the
doorway. The Duchess had arrived,
unannounced. She was on the lookout
for some excitement.

48

'Who *is* that?' said Lady Celia to
Mr Badger, who had just brought her
a special cup of tea.

'Her grace, the Duchess de la Dodo,'
replied Mr Badger.

'Never heard of her,' snapped Lady
Celia as she squinted at the Duchess,
adjusting her glasses. 'I can't put my
finger on it, but there *is* something
familiar about her. Dreadful manners,
I must say, wearing sunglasses indoors.
A very nice fur she is wearing, though –
it reminds me of one I used to wear.
Hmmm, and the shoes, too.'

Mr Badger and Miss Pims watched as the Duchess, spotting an uneaten raspberry-meringue pie with pineapple coulis, set off towards the sweets trolley.

*Clomp, clomp, clomp* went her feet as she strode into the room. Despite those long, long legs, Mr Badger noticed that the Duchess did not move very gracefully.

If it hadn't have been for Mr Badger's quick thinking, what happened next would have made the morning newspapers, if not the *International Philatelic News*. For, with a dreadful squeak and then a shriek, the Duchess de la Dodo slipped on the beautifully re-polished Boubles Grand Hotel Ballroom floor.

Gasping in astonishment, the stamp-collectors looked up as the Duchess became airborne, her extra-long legs flailing above their heads. Her arms flapped about like a great big bird, fanning hats off heads and menus off tables. Most distressing of all, stamps flew everywhere as she struggled to steady herself.

The guests were momentarily stunned into silence. Then the crowd screamed as one as the Duchess – who they only knew as a very tall woman – lurched back mid-air, right into the newly restored Boubles Grand Hotel chandelier.

'*Looks like an attention-seeker,*' *said Lady Celia.*

Back and forth she swayed, suspended by her magnificent hair like a great gangly spider. It was a truly horrifying spectacle. Everyone clutched their seats, as thousands of precious stamps fluttered about the Boubles Grand Hotel Ballroom.

Then, bit by bit, the Duchess —
literally — began to fall apart.

First one long leg, and then another,
dropped to the floor with a loud,
echoing *thud*. Moans filled the room as,
straight after that dreadful scene, the
Duchess's head and hair separated, her
sunglasses flew off and she plunged
to the floor with a crash, right in
front of Sir Cecil and Lady Smothers-
Carruthers. Her grace's hair, though,
was left hanging in the chandelier.

'Good heavens! I *thought* she reminded me of someone!' said Lady Celia, breaking a shocked silence.

'Remarkable,' mumbled Sir Cecil, scratching his head.

For, lying on the floor at their feet, surrounded by stamps, was their darling little granddaughter, Sylvia Smothers-Carruthers.

Mr Badger, sensing that the reputation of the Boubles Grand Hotel was at stake, stepped forward and applauded enthusiastically. 'BRAVO!' he cried.

Following Mr Badger's lead, the whole Philatelic Society joined in with thunderous applause, believing that this performance had all been part of the evening's entertainment, compliments of Sir Cecil and Lady Celia – sort of a spectacular stamp mix-and-match.

*Lady Celia was not amused.*

Mr Badger's quick thinking had saved little Sylvia – in fact the whole Smothers-Carruthers family – from a dreadful embarrassment.

'She's training to be in a circus,' said Lady Celia with a tense smile to some very important stamp-collectors at the next table. 'Isn't she talented?'

# CHAPTER 9

# A Stamp of
# Approval

'You have quite a bit of explaining to do, young lady,' said Lady Celia to a surly Sylvia. 'How did you get your hands on my fur? Not to mention my shoes and my glasses!'

Lady Celia was painfully aware of Sylvia's constant attention-seeking, and it was true that Sylvia desired to be a circus acrobat. 'A clown is more like it,' Lady Celia would hurrumph. 'There'll be no acrobats in this family.'

Mr Badger felt it best not to say anything about Sylvia's occupation of the Royal Suite, not even the three television sets, the food, the drinks or the pizzas, and *especially* not the cake flown down from Edinburgh.

*Someone was a naughty girl.*

Sylvia was in enough trouble as it was, and he did not wish to cause Sir Cecil or Lady Celia any more anxiety.

'Come and sit!' demanded Lady Celia, one hand pointing at the empty seat

next to her and the other at her very
grumpy granddaughter. 'And take off
those earrings.'

While Mr Badger quietly directed
staff to gather up Sylvia's stilts, retrieve
her big wig from the chandelier and
collect her extra-long frock extension
from the floor, Sylvia made herself
comfortable and looked over the
Philatelic Society's special menu,
as if nothing out of the ordinary had
taken place.

63

*Sylvia joined Lady Celia for dessert.*

'You've missed the main course, but you may order dessert,' Lady Celia snapped. 'I'm sure the kitchen would be more than happy to prepare something *very* special for you.'

64

Down below, deep in the Boubles Grand Hotel kitchen, the red-alert light flashed on once again.

Meanwhile, the stamp-collectors were in a state of extreme excitement. Never before had a stamp-swapping evening been as thrilling, resulting in so many unexpected discoveries.

*An extreme excitement of stamp-collectors.*

'Well done, Mr Badger,' whispered
a grateful Sir Cecil with a wink.

'Happy to be of service, sir.'

Mr Badger took the evening's events
in his stride. After all, he *was* the
Boubles Grand Hotel's Special Events
Manager – and this had certainly been
a special event. In fact, the whole day
had been special. Mr Badger had a
feeling that the kitchen staff would
agree.

## CHAPTER 10

# A Cup of Cocoa
# and a Chat

Much later, after Sylvia Smothers-Carruthers had been safely deposited home and tucked into her very own bed, and the Royal Suite had been cleared of pizza boxes, comic books and the three televisions, Mr Badger went home; his work, for today at least, was done.

The Boubles Grand Hotel Royal Suite was ready once more for a royal visitor – hopefully a real one next time.

By the time Mr Badger arrived home, baby Badger and darling daughter Berenice were fast asleep. But not so Mrs Badger.

She was waiting up with hot cocoa and sandwiches to share with her husband.

Mrs Badger was eager to hear about the day's events. And it must be said that Mr Badger took a great delight in relating them to her, for it was not every day that the Philatelic Society Annual Dinner featured a guest as memorable as the Duchess de la Dodo.

A little later, just before he closed his eyes and fell asleep, Mr Badger smiled as he wondered just what he would find in his diary tomorrow morning at the Boubles Grand Hotel.

### The End

More Leigh Hobbs books for you
to enjoy from Allen & Unwin

*Horrible Harriet*
*Hooray for Horrible Harriet*
*4F for Freaks*
*Freaks Ahoy*
*Old Tom's Big Book of Beauty*
*Mr Chicken Goes to Paris*
and of course the Mr Badger books

For more details, visit Leigh's website:
**www.leighhobbs.com.au**

Collect all of *Mr Badger's* adventures
at the Boubles Grand Hotel.

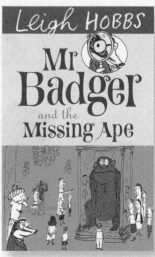

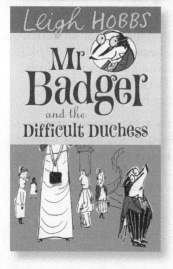

## *A Little More about the Author*

Leigh Hobbs didn't like reading stories very much
when he was a child, though he does remember
adoring *Kidnapped* and *Treasure Island*.

This may seem a disturbing admission for an author
to make but it is not really, because what he *did* like
reading were true stories about other people's lives,
and books about history. These were what fed his
imagination – and in fact continue to do so.

Leigh always wanted to be an artist, so took a special
interest in the pictures. Consequently, he was forever
drawing pictures of castles, knights, pirates and sailing
ships with surprisingly accurate depictions of how
a knight dressed or what a castle looked like.